CHRISTMAS IN BRIARWOOD

A Montana Gallagher Novella
Tales from Briarwood

During a season of hope and healing, two souls find
an unexpected gift in love.

Trappers Peak Publishing
Bigfork, Montana 59911
www.mkmcclintock.com

Publisher's Note: This is a work of fiction. Names, characters, places, and incidents are a product of the author's imagination. Locales and public names are sometimes used for atmospheric purposes. Any resemblance to actual people, living or dead, or to businesses, companies, events, institutions, or locales is completely coincidental.

Christmas in Briarwood; novella/MK McClintock
LARGE PRINT EDITION

Cover Design by MK McClintock

To learn more about MK McClintock and her books,
please visit www.mkmcclintock.com.

For Maddy, Kenzie, and Katie.

Dearest Reader,

The Gallaghers and the wonderful townsfolk of Briarwood are my family, and it brings us tremendous joy every time we can welcome friends, old and new, into our clan. We have come a long way since *Gallagher's Pride*, and we have shared many wonderful adventures, from shoot-outs and kidnappings to second chances in love and life.

Christmas in Briarwood is a story of hope, healing, and realizing that within each of us, is someone deserving of a beautiful life filled with love and friendship. Rachel Watson and Julian Frank are two deserving souls who find a home among the people of Briarwood.

I have written this book to stand on its own. You will meet previous characters and read mention of events from the first seven Montana Gallagher books. They are here to enhance Rachel and Julian's story, for neither would have his or her own tale without those who came before.

Whether you are here for the first time or returning to Briarwood and Hawk's Peak, the Gallaghers and I thank you for joining us on the journey.

Be well, be kind, and stay bookish!
~MK McClintock

CHRISTMAS IN BRIARWOOD

Briarwood, December 8, 1885

FROST NIPPED HER reddening nose, and a crisp breeze brushed her cheeks as the winter sun shined through two puffy white clouds.

Life, she reasoned, was not about achieving happiness for the whole of one's existence, but to enjoy the moment—for it might be the last. Rachel Watson once believed in hope for the future, and never more than now did she long to believe in it again.

Snow dust glistened through the air to land on and around her as she passed beneath the long branches of a tall pine.

With the snow came a scent she had yet been able to describe since winter came to Briarwood. The fragrance of earth and air, light and dark—no matter what time of day or night she strolled the dirt roads, the sweet and refreshing smell grounded her.

In those moments when she thought herself unable to stay and face the events since her arrival, the wide valley and thick, green forests, with soaring mountains beyond, steadied her spirit.

More than the landscape kept her sane, she admitted. The people waved hello, smiled whenever she passed, and invited her into their homes. Although she avoided accepting many of the invitations—save for those at Hawk's Peak or with Doctor Brody and his wife—they continued to make the offers. It's what friends do, she imagined. Her job as a governess in San Francisco had left little time for friendships beyond the staff and her sister, Mary. She thought of all the years spent caring for another couple's children, and wondered, somewhat guiltily, if they hadn't been wasted.

Pine boughs and red ribbon adorned many of the storefronts, and the spicy fragrance of Tilly's apple cider wafted from the café. The faint melody of song carried from the church choir, which practiced the carols it would sing around the town tree. With less than three weeks until Christmas and the opening of the inn, Rachel pictured the grand tree—described in detail by the storekeeper and his wife—covered with homemade ornaments.

Rachel navigated her way up the stone path to the wide front porch of The Briarwood Inn and stopped. A pile of lumber and snow blocked the doorway, so she walked instead to the back door, all the while smiling.

"Oh, wonderful. You're here." Katharine stood on the covered back deck that, when three feet of snow did not cover the ground, allowed for a view of the creek and the mountain range in two directions.

"The front door is blocked."

"One of the builders caught the Smith boys trying to sneak in this morning."

Rachel laughed. "It's no wonder, with all the secrecy. You've piqued everyone's imagination as to what is going on inside."

Katharine held the door open and waved Rachel inside. "It's a hotel. No, not even a hotel. A well-appointed inn. There isn't much mystery in it."

"You'll be chasing off the boys again—and others I'm sure—until you open the place." Rachel set down her cloth-covered basket and unwrapped the thick white scarf from around her neck. "It is looking splendid." She removed the cloth to reveal an assortment of muffins. "I stopped at Tilly's for breakfast, and she asked me to bring these over for the workers. She knows you're not starving because your husband has more sense than to let you go without a meal."

When Katharine raised a brow, with a fresh pecan muffin in hand, Rachel tried not to smile too much. "Tilly's words, not mine." She hung her scarf and decided it was warm enough inside the inn's kitchen to add her long, wool coat to the same hook. "I'm honored to be among the few who get to enter before your grand opening, but I am curious *why* I get the privilege."

"I am going to work up to answering your question. In the meantime, would you help me distribute coffee and these muffins to the men working upstairs? There are three today, and they are almost done with the last bathing room upstairs."

Rachel almost dropped the tin coffee pot before she could pour the strong brew through a strainer into the silver pot Katharine had set out. "Indoor plumbing? Here?"

Katharine nodded. "I fretted over it while they drew the plans up. The hot and cold running water wasn't going to be an issue since others here have managed it, but sending guests to an outdoor privy . . .

well, that wouldn't do. I didn't think it was possible until Brenna Gallagher mentioned the man who was installing a similar system at the ranch. I wish I could say that I knew how it all worked . . . suffice to say there are suspended tanks, pull chains, and great lengths of wood pipes going from the building to, well, out there." Katharine waved toward an empty expanse of land beyond the trees.

Rachel's laugh prevented her from finishing her task without splashing a little coffee on the table. She set the pot down and found a cloth to soak up the mess. "You might recall that I came from San Francisco, though I should like to see your expression again."

"Right, of course." Katharine placed half a dozen muffins on a plate. "We enjoyed some modern amenities in Astoria, but you are used to a far more sophisticated life than anyone else in town, I'm sure." Her voice lost its amusement. "Have you heard from Mary?"

Rachel filled a third tin mug with coffee and set the pot aside. The intentional delay gave her time to force back the start of tears that always threatened to fall when she thought of her sister. "A letter arrived yesterday, in fact, and she cabled last week."

Katharine hesitated before asking, "Is she well?"

"As well as can be." Rachel fought every day to forget what had happened to both her and Mary when their journey to Montana turned from an adventure to an unimaginable nightmare. "She is living with our aunt. Before the weather cooled too much, she visited the beach almost daily. Sometimes I still feel the salt air and smell fish from the day's catch by the wharf."

"Do you miss it?"

How many times had Rachel asked herself that question since she watched her sister board the train bound to the coast? "Some days I do, but most of the time I can't find the words to explain why I stay."

Katharine touched a hand gently on Rachel's arm. "Our circumstances were not the same, and yet, I understand what you mean. It took the thought of not seeing Finn again to admit why I wanted to remain in Briarwood."

Rachel thought of Doctor Finnegan Brody, the man who had saved her life and soon after became a trusted friend. She had only known him as one half of a pair with Katharine, and she could not imagine either without the other. Her ruminations then shifted of their own accord to Julian Frank, the Pinkerton who kept his promise and saved her sister.

"Rachel?"

She looked at Katharine, who now stood in the kitchen doorway with the tray of coffee mugs.

"Did you hear me?"

With Julian's face flitting through her mind, Rachel nodded and picked up the plate of muffins. "Wait. You haven't yet told me why I am here."

"No, I haven't." Katharine indicated the wide staircase leading to the second floor. "Let's pass these around and then how about a tour of the place?"

With her curiosity growing, Rachel followed her friend across the spacious foyer to the stairs.

"Will you spend Christmas in Briarwood now?" Amanda Stuart asked.

Wife to Ben Stuart, the foreman at Hawk's Peak, Amanda had become one of Katharine's dearest friends since moving to the valley. Rachel considered herself blessed to call many at the Hawk's Peak ranch her friends.

"We will. Brody has fretted about leaving the town without a doctor for so long, especially with winter so harsh already." Katharine removed a vase from the final crate her father had brought with him from Astoria. Most of the large wooden boxes contained belongings, but the last two included favorite items from around the seaside house where Katharine had grown up. It was fitting that the mementos would now grace her own home.

Amanda placed a lid back on the empty crate. "At least you had that week in Denver for your honeymoon."

Katharine grinned in return. "Yes. Yes, we did. Though I daresay we saw little of Denver." The women laughed as Katharine found a place for the crystal vase on her new fireplace mantel. "He had his heart set on showing me Ireland, but he won't go so far until he can find another doctor to stay on. Hopefully, in the spring. I heard we aren't the only ones who have delayed a holiday across the sea."

Amanda's raised brow didn't require her question to be verbalized.

"When Eliza was in last week, she mentioned something about Ethan and

Brenna visiting Scotland next year, and not wanting to put it off any longer."

Amanda nodded with new understanding. "Every time they plan to go, life makes other plans for them. Brenna feels Victoria is now old enough to withstand the crossing, so they've talked of going in the spring."

Rachel listened to the women chatter while she unpacked a picture frame and set it on a small table between two stuffed chairs covered in tweed. The polished silver square framed a photograph of a beautiful woman who shared Katharine's eyes and hair, leaving no doubt to their relation.

Katharine and Finnegan Brody had saved her life. Were it not for the skilled hands of Doctor Brody and the generous heart of Katharine Kiely—now Brody— Rachel's story might have had a different ending.

"Do you think they'll make it next year?" Katharine asked Amanda. "To Scotland?"

"Brenna has said as much."

Amanda had confessed to Rachel that it was at Christmas two years ago when she fell in love with Ben Stuart. Her journey to the valley she now called home had been an arduous one, filled with a little hope and a lot of desperation. The Gallaghers took a chance on Amanda when she arrived in town, alone and unknown, just as they had Katharine and her grand ideas.

Rachel wondered how many others they'd rescued and brought into their lives. She supposed she was now counted among the lost, weary, and orphaned embraced by the Gallagher family and the people of Briarwood. She often thought how alike Ethan Gallagher and Brody were with their fierce sense of responsibility to others.

"Are you all right?"

Rachel heard the question twice before realizing it was meant for her. She nodded to Amanda. "Thinking is all. Is the last crate empty?"

"It is, thank heavens. Brody emptied the

heavier items last night." Katharine wiped a speck of dust from the vase and scanned their progress. "Thank you both for helping today."

"I've enjoyed the company." Amanda folded the wool blanket that had protected the crystal.

"As have I." Rachel tapped the edge of the picture frame once before turning away. "You and Brody have built a beautiful home. I can imagine a grand Christmas tree right there in front of the window, with the snow falling behind."

"It is a perfect spot." Generous windows broke up sturdy walls of smooth-cut timbers in the expansive great room. Katharine told them she had fallen so much in love with Hawk's Peak, and the Gallaghers indulged her when she asked if her architect could use their ranch as inspiration. "All credit goes to our builder. It delayed the inn by several months, but it was worth it, and Brody now has all of his clinic rooms back and available for patients."

"I still find it odd that you call him Brody," Amanda said.

Katharine laughed and tucked the folded blanket Amanda passed her into a trunk in the room's corner. "There is less confusion when I speak of him to others, but he is Finn when we are alone."

Rachel said, "Your father seemed pleased when he was last here."

"Oh, yes. Between the spur line and the new inn, he is quite pleased. Even with the train depot five miles from town, it has proven a worthy investment." With hands on hips, Katharine studied the room. "It has turned out rather nice, hasn't it?"

Amanda ran her fingers over the edge of a polished shelf, now partially covered with books. "It's beautiful. I see the similarities to Hawk's Peak, but you've put your touch on it. Does the inn look anything like this? You have allowed no one inside except the workers."

Katharine and Rachel shared a glance

and a smile. Rachel already had the pleasure of touring the impressive interior yet reminded herself to ask again why she was given such an honor before everyone else. Her friend had managed to avoid answering before it was time for them to come here to meet Amanda.

"It's supposed to be a surprise. My father suggested we hire someone from San Francisco or Chicago to decorate, but I have enjoyed doing it myself."

"And how is that going?"

Katharine chuckled and led the way from the great room to the kitchen. "I may have taken on more than I bargained."

Rachel wanted to keep her hands busy and had to stop herself from preparing the tea in her friend's home. She still wasn't used to others doing for her. "Folks have noticed wagons full of deliveries."

Katharine nodded. "Yes, and there's more to come, but we will have most of the furniture made here."

"At the Petersen farm." Amanda grinned

at her friend. "You didn't think that would be kept secret, did you?"

"How long have you known?"

"Since the beginning, I expect. It is safe to assume that most everyone knows. When the Petersen's last crop failed, they planned to leave the area. Not only did they stay, but they also hired on half a dozen men. Why keep it quiet?"

Katharine put the kettle on the stove for the water to heat. "It seemed unnecessary to mention. The men have work they can be proud of, and truly, it would cost more to ship furniture in. It was a business decision, and if it helps Hugh Petersen build his business, then I am happy to help."

Not *only* business, Rachel thought. Katharine was not one to draw attention to her good deeds. Rachel had learned over the months that everyone she had met in town gave as much of themselves as they could, without expecting recognition in return. Amanda must have understood because she shifted her attention to the man under topic.

"How did you know Hugh Petersen built furniture?" Amanda asked. "I've lived here for two years and did not know."

Katharine's shoulders lifted in a dainty shrug. "Brody. He mentioned once that with Hugh's poor farmland, he ought to switch to woodworking. Brody also shared that Hugh had built a few of the pieces in the clinic, and the workmanship was impressive."

"Still, the inn must be taking a tremendous amount of your time, and it hasn't even opened. And with all your work helping Brody at the clinic . . . you don't have to do it all alone."

"Amanda's right," Rachel said. "It must be a lot of work."

"It was arrogant for me to think I could. Please, both of you have a seat. We've earned a respite." Katharine pulled down three teacups with saucers and her favorite Wedgewood teapot, which had once belonged to her mother, checked the kettle, and decided the water was hot enough. Placing a combination of dried herbs and flowers in the teapot, she let the herbs steep for a minute.

"Is there much left to do?" Amanda asked. "And what about when you open? You can't think to manage the inn on your own."

Katharine gave her friend an indulgent smile. "If I didn't already know how busy you were at the ranch, Amanda—and with your own household—I would think you were looking for a job."

Amanda's light laugh accompanied a shake of her head. "I'll be busier come spring."

The glance, followed by a studied perusal of her friend's face, shifted Katharine and Rachel's attention. "You are?" Both women simultaneously asked the same question.

"I am."

Katharine enveloped Amanda's hands

and squeezed. "Brody is officially the best keeper of secrets this town will ever know."

"Which is why we all trust him. He confirmed it last month, but I wanted to wait before telling anyone." Amanda sobered. "Ben and I have come close twice before, and I couldn't bear to make it real until I was certain."

"And are you certain this time?"

"The good doctor said I am in perfect health, and I'm much farther along than ever before."

"Spring." Katharine guessed at a time frame. "We'll certainly wait until the baby comes before going to Ireland."

Amanda shook her head. "There will always be expectant mothers, broken bones, and mysterious illnesses. Don't let any of it stop you from living your life. Speaking of life in motion, let's get back to the inn?"

"Your news is far more exciting, and we'll give it proper celebration later. As for the inn, there's not too much left. Thankfully, the exterior, piping, and most of the interior were completed before the first snow. The builder estimates two more weeks to finish, which means not a day to spare before we prepare for the Christmas party. Many others could oversee things now to give me more time with Brody and at the clinic, and I trust the builder, but it would be handy to have someone—"

"I'd like to help."

Amanda held the knife above the coffee cake as she looked at Katharine before both women faced Rachel. "Would you really?" Katharine asked.

"I would." Rachel took pride in her work at the general store and appreciated all Loren and Joanna Baker had done for her, but increasingly, she found herself with too much time to remember. She needed to keep busy. Really busy.

Katharine placed a strainer over the first teacup and poured tea from the pot into one cup, then the other two. "I won't turn down your offer, Rachel. Why don't you stop by the inn again this afternoon if you have time? Will two o'clock work?"

"Again?" Amanda asked.

"I gave Rachel a tour this morning." Katharine set one teacup in front of Amanda and acted as though she had said nothing out of the ordinary.

"This morning, you say? And you let me carry on."

Katharine handed Rachel a cup and then sat down to join the other women. "Well, it will still be a surprise."

"Then on behalf of myself, at least, I look forward to the inn's interior unveiling." Amanda sipped her tea and took a small bite of the coffee cake while directing her next question to Rachel. "Will you return to San Francisco to spend Christmas with Mary?"

Rachel held her teacup level with her mouth to hide the thin line of tension. She did not blame anyone for their curiosity. "I have heard the town is at its most beautiful and festive on Christmas day. I look forward to seeing it." She had written as much to Mary in the letter that now lay in her skirt pocket.

Amanda asked, "What are the holidays like in San Francisco? Much the same, I should think."

"Festive, certainly." Rachel enjoyed Christmas, but it had always been just another day. She went to church, ate supper with the children, and shared a cup of warm cider with the other house staff. She spent a few hours every Christmas Eve with her aunt and sister, though often felt rushed to get back to her charges. "The family I worked for did not make a big celebration of Christmas."

"Then you are in for a treat this year," Amanda promised.

Katharine sat in silence for a few seconds before asking no one in particular, "Have you heard anything from Julian Frank?"

Amanda glanced at Rachel first before saying, "As it happens, I have—or, rather,

Ramsey did and he shared it with everyone at the ranch." Amanda stared at the slow rise of steam from her teacup but made no move to touch it or more of her cake. "Julian has returned to the territory."

Rachel had come to know everyone at Hawk's Peak well since her arrival more than a year before, including Ramsey. Eliza's husband, a sometimes-acting U.S. Marshal when needed, and a horse breeder alongside his wife knew Julian Frank better than anyone else in the valley. "For what purpose?"

Amanda looked directly at Rachel. "Ramsey didn't share all the details. He said only that Julian returned, and he has news for you."

Rachel almost choked on her next sip of tea. "What news, and why did he not write or cable me directly?"

"I don't know, Rachel. I swear I would tell you if I did, but it seems Julian swore Ramsey to secrecy on whatever else he revealed."

Katharine stood, cleared away her cup and half-eaten cake, and poured the rest of her tea into the washbasin. "Rachel has more of a right to know than anyone here."

"Please don't be upset on my behalf."

"After everything . . ." Katharine took a deep breath. "I don't know which of them I want to give a good scolding to more, Julian or Ramsey."

"Neither." Rachel crossed the kitchen to take Katharine's hands. A few months ago, she would not have been so bold, and she considered it a significant achievement. "This morning we laughed, and you showed me your beautiful inn. Let us go back to that. Julian will share the news the next time we meet."

"I'm sorry, Rachel." Katharine nodded. "It's just that—"

"I understand." And she did. Katharine had been with her through the recovery, through the uncertainty, and had even become an almost-surrogate sister after Mary left. "It is time for me to fight my own battles, from wherever they may come. Besides, I trust Julian, and if he needs to tell me the news himself, then I'll wait."

Amanda left the table to stand next to her friends. "Julian's telegram specifically said he would be here by week's end."

Katharine nodded and pumped water into the basin. "Well, Rachel and I have plenty to keep ourselves busy at the inn until then." Katharine stopped pumping water and faced Rachel. "How long has it been since Julian was last here? Three months?"

"Four." Four months, one week, and three days, to be exact. Rachel kept the by-day tally of Julian's lengthy absence to herself. He stuck around only two days on his last visit to Briarwood. A month before that, it had been one day. She often asked herself why he bothered to return for such brief visits. Briarwood was not his home, though she always hoped she'd see him again, regardless.

"Ethan happens to agree with you, Katharine, which is why he read the telegram and rode into town with me and Ben this morning." Amanda wiped the table of a few stray crumbs. "Ethan and Ben said they would come by here after a stop at the livery and general store."

Fierce pounding echoed into the kitchen and propelled Katharine to the front door. On the other side, Loren Baker's hand was raised to knock again. "Loren, whatever is wrong?"

The older man huffed before asking, "Where's Doc Brody?"

"At the Fenton farm. Mrs. Fenton had a difficult delivery. He's been there all night."

"I'll go and find Ben. He can ride out to fetch the doctor." Amanda pulled her coat from a row of hooks and slipped her arms into the sleeves. She followed with a thick knitted scarf and wool hat.

"No, I'll go. In this weather and in your condition, if you fell, Ben wouldn't forgive any of us," Katharine said. "Come in, Loren. What's happened?"

"Joanna fell climbing a ladder she shouldn't have been on. She says she is fine, but I won't rest until the doc has a look at her and tells me himself."

The door opened again and would have slammed against the wall had Brody not kept a firm grip on the handle. He closed the door quickly behind him but made no move to discard his outer clothes.

"Katharine, what's—" Red-faced and breathing heavily, Brody asked, "Loren, are you here for me?"

"It's Joanna."

Katharine reached for her heavy wool coat and scarf. "I'll go with you."

Brody put a hand on his wife's shoulder. "Not this time. The weather is worsening faster than expected. Even between here and the general store, the road is barely visible. I saw Ben and Ethan a few minutes ago, and they'll be along soon to fetch Amanda. Please, you and Rachel stay here until I return."

Rachel knew Katharine wanted to argue with Brody's decision, but refrained, especially in front of the others. Going where he was needed—wherever someone required a healer's touch—was Brody's calling, and expecting him to do otherwise would be the same as demanding he become someone other than the wonderful, dedicated man and doctor Katharine loved.

Katharine stood on her toes and pressed a hard kiss to her husband's lips. "Be careful." She opened the door to a flurry of snow. Brody braced himself against the rising wind and followed Loren back into the icy air.

Julian recalled the day he had met Rachel with vivid detail. Strength had lurked beneath the anxious and fragile exterior as she fought against worry for her sister. He remembered not a word of concern for herself had passed her lips.

And not once did she ask about the man who kidnapped and hurt both her and Mary. Julian, however, never stopped thinking about Slade Ryker. Blizzards and impassable mountain trails kept Julian from following in person, so he hunted from afar, sending telegrams to every sheriff, marshal, and deputy in the Rocky Mountains.

He investigated every possible sighting himself, from Colorado to Canada, with each search ending in disappointment. Any criminal wishing to flee their fate could lose themselves in the vast wildernesses of the Rocky Mountains, and Slade's early start had given him an advantage. Slade's luck finally ran out two weeks ago.

Julian tossed out half a dozen starts to a letter explaining what happened. He then considered sending a telegram before he returned to the life of a Pinkerton. Rachel deserved better from him—deserved to hear him say the words.

She smiled for the first time in their acquaintance when he rode through four months ago. Her brilliant light shined through the sadness and dazzled him as no smile—no woman—ever had. Julian kept his attraction and affection buried deep, believing her not ready. His visit had been brief, but he needed to know she was all right, to see her with his own eyes. Ramsey kept him informed with regular telegrams, and yet, it was never enough.

Long legs, strong from years of riding horses and walking mountain trails, carried Julian across the snow-dusted road to the thicker drifts near the small church. After kicking each boot lightly against the other to clean them from excess snow, he opened the door and quietly entered.

She was the only one inside. Julian closed the door with a soft click and stood by the entrance for a minute, not wishing to disturb her. Rachel sat with her head bowed, and only when she raised it and turned to look out a window did Julian make his presence known.

"Miss Watson." He spoke her name with reverence, and barely above a whisper, but she heard him. With each step down the aisle between long benches on either side, his boots resounded on the wood floor of the church.

"You stayed away longer this time."

She didn't look at him when she spoke, and he liked to think she'd recognize his voice under any circumstances. "I had something to finish before I could return." Julian made himself comfortable in the pew in front of where she sat and rested his arm on the bench back. The afternoon sun glowed through the church windows, casting an ethereal glimmer throughout the interior. It had been seventeen years since he had set foot inside a church, and only Rachel's presence had possessed him to enter one now. Odd, he thought, how comfortable it seemed after such a long absence.

"Is it finished then?"

"It is." Julian wished his brain and mouth would start working together. He'd played out in mind what to say, and now that he was in the same room with her, he wanted to talk about anything except what brought him here. "You aren't going to ask what or how?"

"You'll tell me if you want to."

Perhaps, Julian mused, she wasn't ready. "I reckon I will. I'm still working out how best to tell you, though, and that might take a while longer than I first figured."

Rachel glanced his way. "You're an unusual man, Julian Frank."

"I'll accept that as a compliment."

"I meant it as one, even though you can be also an exasperating man."

Julian found little to smile about most days, but a few minutes in Rachel's company always gave him a reason. "I've been told. What brought you into church on a Friday?"

"The same thing that urged you, I imagine."

"Doubtful, since I'm here only because you are."

The confession rendered her momentarily silent. "Are you always so honest?"

"Only to people who deserve honesty."

"And the rest of the people?"

Julian shrugged. "They deserve whatever's coming to them. I can leave if you'd rather be alone."

Rachel shook her head. "Did you know the reverend here does not identify with any one religion? He was raised a Quaker and teaches from the Bible, but he believes faith is a never-ending journey—his words—and that what a person believes in their heart is between them and God."

"What of those who believe nothing?"

She smiled. "When I asked him the same thing, he told me that's part of the never-ending journey. I don't know what I believe anymore."

Julian believed in God and miracles because he'd seen too much to doubt the presence of power no human on earth could ever understand. Beyond that, he believed . . . now it was his turn to be struck silent. "Again, what brought you here today?"

"A prayer for Joanna Baker. She fell off a ladder. Brody said she's fine, and a few days' rest will see her right. Loren showed up at the clinic in such a panic, I thought it might have been more serious."

"Love can make a man crazy."

"I suppose." Rachel relaxed a bit more. "Mary and I used to attend services every Sunday. Our employer expected it of all in her employ. This is the first time I've been inside a church since I came to Briarwood."

Julian knew too well what she'd left unsaid—she hadn't been in a church since Slade Ryker. "You'll never be the person you were before."

She choked on a quick laugh that

stemmed from surprise. "You are the only one to say that directly to me, though Doctor Brody came close. They all know it, though."

"Of course, they do." Julian adjusted his body so he could look at her better. "I know little about the people around here, but I've heard things from Ramsey and others. You don't go through everything the Gallaghers have endured without a lot of scars."

"The Gallaghers all seem so levelheaded, like nothing can ever touch them."

"People learn to live with the scars, and eventually the scars fade to make room for positive memories that are stronger than the wounds. You've made friends here, have found reasons to laugh with them, and whether or not you realize it, you're building a life here now."

"Ramsey keeps you well informed, doesn't he? It's true, I've been fortunate and have made friends. It's impossible not to. People in Briarwood are kind, and I needed kindness more than I admitted to myself." Rachel stared at him for several seconds before saying, "Forgive me. You sound like a man who has scars of his own."

"Never met a man or woman who doesn't have scars." He leaned toward her. "Everyone falls at some point, Rachel, willingly or not. The difference between those who stay fallen and those who rise is the courage to keep going when everything else seems impossible."

Three tears, one after the other, slid down her pale cheeks. "Some days it's harder to rise and be courageous than others."

"As the reverend told you, it's a journey." Julian stood and stepped back. The desire to hold out his hand and offer it to her for support was fierce. He made a fist instead to keep the desire in check. "I'd like to show you something if you're of a mind to join me."

Julian remained sitting until Rachel

decided if she wanted to go with him. When she finally stood, he immediately joined her and allowed her to walk ahead of him. He enjoyed watching the way she went from small hesitations in her movements to standing straighter, with her shoulders back and head high. He passed her only long enough to open the church door.

Once outside, she stopped, looked around, and after he said nothing, gave him a pointed look. "Well?"

He smiled in response to her unexpected sass. Her tears had dried, yet her eyes remained bright. "What are you wearing on your feet?"

"My feet?"

"I could explain—"

"Boots."

"Warm socks?"

"Woolen. What is the fascination with my footwear?"

Julian's quick smile prompted a like reaction from Rachel. "I've never seen frostbite myself, but Doc Brody described it once in detail. I'd just as soon you avoid an amputation.

She narrowed her eyes at him. "Where are we going?"

Because she needed details—needed control—Julian said, "It's two miles west of town. The sun is out, and it's not as cold right now, so we have a window. Some sunlight will do you good."

She turned away from the door to look at him. "You've only just returned. Shouldn't you rest?"

"Where we're going is plenty restful, even in winter."

They walked first to the general store, where they stopped at the front counter first. Rachel waited for Loren to finish with a customer before she asked, "How is Joanna?"

"According to her, she is fit to run the store, me, and the town without issue. According to Doc Brody, she's to stay abed for two more days." He winked at Rachel.

"I'm thinking my wife will win this round."

Rachel and Julian both smiled. "She sounds herself then." Rachel watched Julian wander the store and stop at a display of winter goods. "If you will please excuse me for a moment, Loren." She walked to Julian's side. "You are in need of new gloves?"

"No, you are." Julian picked out a thicker pair of gloves than the ones Rachel currently wore and asked Loren to put it on his account. He'd opened the account at the general store the day before, which is when Loren had welcomed him back to Briarwood. Julian thought it an indication of a single root planted and a sign he would be in Briarwood more than a few days this time.

He added an extra thick scarf for good measure and waited while Rachel put everything on. Grateful Rachel missed Loren's amusement at their interchange, he thanked the shopkeeper, asked Loren to give Joanna his good wishes, and walked outside with Rachel.

Side by side, they crossed the road to the livery. Julian caught and held her arm when she slipped on a small patch of ice. "You all right?"

Rachel nodded. "Thanks to you, I didn't humiliate myself with an ungraceful tumble to the ground."

"Nothing wrong with a tumble now and then." Julian released her arm and whispered to his horse. "This is Ransom," he said, when Rachel reached out to brush her hand over the gelding's nose. Without checking with the blacksmith, Julian saddled a second mount for Rachel. "Ransom wouldn't mind both of us for a short distance, but I figure you'd prefer to ride alone."

She did, but how did he know? Rachel accepted his help into the saddle, and at the last second, she sat astride. Her long wool skirt fell past the top of her boots and kept her legs warm. If Julian thought the position unladylike, he didn't say. Rachel thought she might have even seen him smile again.

They kept to the road for fifteen minutes before Julian led her onto a trail that wound through trees. The burble of water went unseen, but its welcoming sound reminded her that life flowed no matter the season or circumstance. Rachel finally made out a trail on the ground below as it appeared periodically through the thinner layers of snow.

Only someone who knew the land well could have known of its existence. She watched Julian, with his straight back and easy stride, as he and his horse moved as one. Snow dust drifted from the pine boughs, captured by shimmers of sunlight. She inhaled deeply and tilted her head back to capture their essence on her skin.

"We're almost there."

Rachel opened her eyes to see no change in the landscape unless she shifted slightly in the saddle to look past Julian. The woods parted, and beyond . . . she could not form the proper words to describe what lay before her. "The Valley of Dreams."

Julian waited until she and her horse stood beside him before speaking. "Not quite. It flows into The Valley of Dreams, but this place is different. The area is traditionally common hunting ground for the tribes with Blackfeet to the north, Crow to the east, and Pend d'Orielle and Salish to the west, and more beyond. Keme, a Blackfoot warrior I met fifteen years past in this spot, said this place has no name because its purpose in someone's life is not known until they gaze upon it and hear Earth speak."

"Has it ever spoken to you?"

"Once."

Julian did not explain, and Rachel did not ask. She longed to dismount and walk the land, to feel the earth's vibrations beneath her soles. Instead, she remained in the saddle and urged the horse forward until they left the canopy of trees. December's sun burned bright between two heavy clouds and touched down on the valley floor. Life beyond the trees and sky and frosted grasses remained hidden, and loathe to disturb an unsuspecting creature's peace, she did not venture farther.

A prayer came unbidden, filling mind and heart. Words for Mary, who she prayed had found peace at home with their aunt, and thoughts for Doctor Brody, whose knowledge and skill she was thankful for daily. The thoughts and prayers continued as faces of each new friend faded in and out of her mind. Her silent supplication for strength, courage, and hope ended abruptly with a plea for revenge.

When she returned to her senses and regained her bearings, she found Julian's gaze in avid study. His eyes asked more than he could have said with words alone, and when he did not speak, Rachel released the tightness in her chest. She had been quiet long enough for the sun to drift behind neighboring clouds, as though its light could no longer be shared when her thoughts had turned so dark.

Revenge.

"Rachel?"

His gloved hand hovered close to hers. He wanted to touch, to comfort, to share his strength. This much she sensed, and yet, she could not accept. Not yet. Not with her heart so filled with . . . not hate exactly, but a darkness. She painted a mental image of the valley, surrounded by pine-covered mountains on one side, and a rocky expanse of cliff on the other.

"Look."

She followed to where Julian pointed and somehow, for a moment, pain made room once again for joy. A small herd of wild horses numbering only seven crossed the valley and stopped to bend their heads, some partaking of water while the others kept watch. Nature hid the stream from their view, but droplets of the earth's gift fell when each horse raised its head. "I am surprised they come during the winter months."

"It's rare to see them this time of year," Julian said. "Animals know water is here, and it is their lifeblood. The horses use their hooves to paw through snow and find vegetation beneath. They, too, are survivors."

Rachel continued to watch, and when they did not move on, she said to Julian, "I'm ready to go back." When he turned his horse around and faced her, Rachel touched the edge of his coat sleeve. "How did you know this place spoke to you?"

Julian kept his eyes on her, instead of the valley, when he replied. "When the need for revenge left my heart."

"Did it last?" She glimpsed darkness enter the depths of Julian's hazel eyes.

"For a time."

"Revenge fills mine," she confessed. "I thought it gone, or at least tempered enough for me to move on. I do not think of him as much as I used to. It's odd that such a wondrous place brought back the helplessness and hopelessness. I have been feeling . . ." her eyes watered. "Chaos lives inside me. One moment I believe happiness is within reach, and the next I can barely breathe."

"It's time now to answer the question you asked me earlier, in the church."

Rachel tightened her grip on the reins. "If it's bad news—"

"Slade Ryker is dead."

They sat atop their horses for several minutes, and not once during that time did Rachel's eyes shift from his. "That is what you had to finish?"

"I made you a promise."

She released an unsteady breath in slow degrees. "How did it happen?"

"Rachel—"

"Tell me. Please, Julian."

"I finally came upon him at a farmer's house in Tennessee, after a lead from a deputy in Wyoming, who had been visiting family out that way. It was luck, pure and simple that the deputy had been in the right place at the right time. Unfortunately, the farmer was already dead when I arrived, as was his wife. They had two daughters, both tied up when I entered the farmhouse."

"Your candor is both welcoming and disturbing in equal measure." She sucked in a breath. "Did he . . . were they harmed?"

Julian shook his head. "He didn't have time before I got there."

Rachel did not need to know the rest, for her imagination had played out every scenario, and in not one of them did she have the courage to kill Slade herself. "If you knew he'd traveled so far, why follow him? Why not wait until he returned?"

"Because, Rachel, I made you a promise."

He walked Ransom closer, removed his right glove, and brushed a tear from her cheek. Rachel hadn't realized she was crying. An almost imperceptible rumble dried her remaining tears. "What is that?"

"Let's go." Julian turned his horse around. "Ride, now. Fast."

"Julian, what's—"

The rumbling increased. "No time." He smacked her horse's rump and set the mare into a run. "Go!" He and Ramson kept as close to the mare as safety allowed, using their combined energy to keep Rachel and her mare at a run. The animals navigated the trees easier than the humans on their backs. Dodging tree branches that weren't there a few minutes ago, they ducked their heads and held fast.

When the trail allowed for it, Julian and Ransom moved alongside Rachel and the mare. They continued until, without warning, Julian guided his horse ahead and slowed Ransom from a gallop to a canter and then finally to a stop. The rumble rolled as snow smashed through a wide swath of trees, breaking branches, and coating the understory with a heavy layer of snow.

Rachel pressed a hand to her breast, just above her racing heart, as though pressing down might slow its rapid beat. "What just happened?"

"Avalanche."

"I've felt the shock of earthquakes in San Francisco, but nothing so close—so raw. What caused it, do you think?"

Julian brushed a gloved hand over Ransom's neck. A thick layer of sweat, despite the cold, darkened patches of the animal's body. "Too much sun, wind, rain, or snow can cause one. There's been heavy snowfall early this year, though an avalanche in this area is unusual. We need to get back and warn folks to stay away from the ridge above."

"What about the horses in the valley?"

"They know what to do."

Rachel looked once more where they had been only moments before. The trail, now completely covered, blocked all view to what lay beyond. "Yes, but they . . . you're certain they are all right?"

"I'm sure." Julian kept to her side as the horses started into a walk. "We'll take it slow the rest of the way."

After Julian's report, talk of the avalanche spread through town, and by nightfall, despite the frigid air and smell of more snow to come, folks gathered at Tilly's Café, where townspeople warmed themselves with conversation and a bowl of Tilly's hearty stew or a thick slice of meat loaf.

After Julian left Rachel at the general store while he tended the horses at the livery, he made his way to the café with the hope she'd be there. He nursed a cup of steaming coffee, until after a third visit from the waitress, ordered a serving of meat loaf and potatoes.

A hush fell over the café's patrons when Gabriel Gallagher strode inside, hung his coat and hat on one of the many hooks made available for such things, and scanned the room. He said hello to every person he passed before stopping at

Julian's table in the back corner. "Do you mind?"

"Not at all." Julian waited for Gabriel to sit and give his order to the waitress who returned as soon as she saw him.

"Thank you, Noreen."

"Noreen. She spoke too fast the first time for me to catch her name." When the waitress left them alone, Julian asked, "You came to town alone?"

Gabriel nodded. "Ben and I were riding the ridge when the avalanche happened. I wanted to warn folks about staying away from that area, so I rode in. Heard right off from Otis at the livery that you and Rachel were out there when it happened."

"That's right. The trees slowed the snow down somewhat and gave us a chance to run it out. Any idea what set it off?"

"Best we can tell is too much snow along the ridge. It's been a hard winter, and we're not even halfway through it. You sure Rachel's all right?"

"She is." Julian had occasion to meet the

Gallagher siblings a few times since Ramsey first asked for his help to locate Rachel's sister last winter. While Ethan was the more serious among them, with the weight of family responsibility weighing heavier on the oldest, Julian thought of Gabriel as the one who probably spent as much time charming women in his youth as he did learning to ranch.

Personally, he'd rather deal with the youngest sibling, Eliza. She cut right through a person with a single look and seemed to know what you were thinking as you thought it. Saved him a lot of time with small talk. He smiled, thinking Ramsey had done well for himself. "Ramsey told me Rachel had grown close to your family. That you're here now asking about her tells me he was right."

"She and Brenna have become especially close, and she likes to spend time with the children." Gabriel drank a long swallow of coffee and looked Julian squarely in the eyes. "Have you told her?"

Julian's response was a single nod.

"Good." He looked around the room as patrons filed out of the café. "Rachel and the avalanche aren't the only reasons I'm here."

"Figured as much."

Gabriel's quick smile highlighted faint lines around his eyes. Talk stopped when Noreen brought their plates out. When they declined anything else, she smiled in parting and hurried over to another table. "You've met Tom Culver, right?"

Julian sifted through his mental cache of people. "Part-time sheriff and former ranch hand at Hawk's Peak."

"That's right. Tom and his son are leaving in a few months. He has a sister in Tucson who recently lost a husband, so they're going down to help her out." Gabriel spooned a helping of stew into his spoon before adding, "Which leaves the town with a vacancy."

Julian sliced into his meat loaf and took his time chewing on both the delicious bite and Gabriel's comment. He used his knife to point at the meat loaf. "There's something in here I can't quite place, but it sure is good."

Gabriel chuckled. "Isabelle swears it's nutmeg, Amanda says it's molasses. My wife is from New Orleans where Tilly also spent time, but Amanda does most of the cooking. I never took sides."

"I have a job, Gabriel."

"A good job, and I'm only putting the offer out there. It's time we had a full-time sheriff, dedicated to the people of this town and the valley, and Ramsey thought you might be interested."

What Ramsey thought, Julian mused, was that Julian wouldn't want to leave Rachel again now that Ryker was dead. Did he want to go? A part of him already hankered to be on the trail again, tracking his next suspect. Another part of him— growing stronger every minute—wanted to stay. "If I have to leave, you'll keep looking after Rachel?"

Gabriel nodded slowly, his smile gone. "She's one of us now."

Julian picked up his fork and knife again and cut off another corner of his meat loaf. "I appreciate your confidence, and I won't make any promises, but I will think on it."

"Sounds fair."

Six days passed before Rachel saw Julian again. Helping Katharine at the inn occupied most of her days, and she found the work rewarding. Each time a new shipment of linens arrived or men from the Petersen farm delivered a new piece of furniture, Rachel and Katharine delighted in the unpacking and placing of items.

A stack of heavy quilts, along with dishes, was delivered this morning. The convenience of the spur line meant only a few miles travel from the station to town. Rachel often wondered what type of people Katharine expected to frequent the cozy inn. With ten rooms, five standard and five luxurious over the top two floors, there would be plenty of room for weary travelers or curious visitors.

The main level featured a small dining room for inn guests only, and a larger common area, where, as Katharine had promised when she sold the idea to the people, town functions and events could be held.

Two laundresses, three maids, and a cook had already been hired for when the inn opened its doors to the public. The season would be short, Katharine warned Rachel, with most guests staying late spring through early autumn, when fairer weather welcomed old friends and strangers alike.

It was Rachel's job to see that the inn ran efficiently and the guests who slept within its walls were comfortable. She admitted, only to herself and in the dark of night, that she might not be up for the job. Possibilities kept her motivated to do her very best for Katharine, the town, and herself.

Christmas, she decided, was going to be unlike any other this year.

A knock at the back door drew Rachel away from unpacking a crate of plates ordered from New York. She expected Hugh Petersen with a sideboard for the dining room. Instead, her surprise was met by Julian with his hand raised and ready to knock again. Whenever he smiled at her, she always felt it was with his eyes as much as his mouth. A gentle warmth spread through her unexpectedly, and she tamped it before her face turned an unbecoming shade of crimson.

"Katharine gave me permission to go as far as the kitchen." Julian grinned. "Unless I can convince you to walk with me."

Rachel thought of all the work awaiting her and then peeked her head farther outside. "I'm not entirely certain people are meant to venture about in such cold. The temperature has dropped since I walked over this morning."

"Just takes a little time for your blood to thicken. Until then, a coat, scarf, hat, and gloves should keep you warm enough. We won't go far." He glanced down at her feet. "And warmer boots."

"The last time you invited me out, we nearly met our end in an avalanche." She regretted the words the moment they fell from her lips. "I didn't mean that the way it sounded."

Julian kept the mood light. "You're not wrong. Anything can happen out there." They sobered at the same time. If anyone knew the risk of getting caught unawares in the wilderness, it was Rachel. "Now it's my turn to apologize."

"Come inside. I won't be long." Rachel disappeared into the room off the kitchen—the room that was hers if she wanted it, Katharine explained—and readied herself for the cold walk ahead. She should have turned down the invitation and kept her distance from Julian Frank.

Rachel relied on him more than she should want. He'd already been in town longer than she expected him to stay. She didn't want to think about the day when he left for good.

She reentered the kitchen, this time covered properly for the excursion. "I had a warmer pair of boots here."

He smiled and opened the door for her. For several minutes, they walked in silence. White and cream on top, and growing progressively darker, the pillowy clouds filled the sky far beyond the mountains. Shadows danced on snowy slopes as sunlight sneaked through the angry clouds, only to be swallowed again into darkness. Rachel doubted a hand skilled enough existed to compete with the flawless brush Nature used to paint her landscapes.

"I feel as though I ask you this too often, but where are we going?"

"Not far. Fresh air and sunlight are good for you."

She glanced up again, then at Julian. "I

daresay you are as good at reading the weather as a broken barometer." Rachel responded to his sideways look with a shrug. "It's dark enough to be confused with early evening."

"Patience, Miss Watson."

He was right about the air. She inhaled its sweet freshness and held it in her lungs for a few seconds before releasing it again.

Julian led her to a bridge that spanned a section of the creek. "Now we wait."

"Wait for what?"

"It helps if you close your eyes."

She giggled. There was no other word for it. Rachel couldn't remember the last time she giggled. "For a second I thought you were going to say, 'It helps if you close your mouth.'" Rachel heard the humor in his next words.

"It's a pleasure to hear you talk, Miss Watson, so you go right ahead and keep at it."

"Why are you back to calling me 'Miss Watson'?"

He avoided the question. "Just keep your eyes closed for a minute longer."

"I feel silly."

"What do you see?"

"Snow. A lot of snow." Rachel lifted her arms in a wide shrug. "I can't see anything, but I already know there is a lot of snow. Everywhere."

"All right. What do you feel?"

Rachel concentrated first on the cold and then pushed beyond it. Something warm caressed her face. She tilted her head back farther. "It can't be." Her eyes opened to ensure her skin had not deceived her. The tumultuous clouds had separated, and in the valley they created in the sky, sunlight spread over the meadow. Its reach expanded until it touched her fully and enveloped them both. She then raised her gaze to stare across the meadow where it led to the distant woods and mountains beyond.

Julian observed her face lest he miss even the most subtle shift of her eyes or twitch of her mouth. His close attention allowed him to witness the moment she lost herself in the snow, the air, the sky, and the ever-changing beauty surrounding her. "How did you know the sun was going to come out?" She looked at him then.

"It always does—eventually."

"Miss Rachel!"

Drawn from nature's solace, Rachel and Julian turned toward the sound of a childish voice. Jacob Gallagher's stubby legs carried him with surprising swiftness over the snow-covered road to the church and meadow, right behind his cousin Andrew. Little huffs of breath hit the cold with each exertion.

Ethan Gallagher strode on longer legs, keeping only a stride's length between him and his son. The proud father wore an indulgent smile, but it was the apparent love Julian witnessed in the man's eyes that made him wonder what he'd missed out on when he chose a life with the Pinkertons rather than settling down with a family.

"Miss Rachel!"

Julian and Rachel walked through the taller snow to meet the new arrivals. Andrew reached them first, and immediately after, Julian stepped forward and in one motion lifted and swung Jacob in the air before he ran into Rachel's legs. "You're faster than your pa's horse."

Jacob giggled and clapped his hands. "Horse!"

Julian set the boy back on the ground and he hurried to his father, who lifted him and held him against his chest.

Andrew handled the explanation for their sudden appearance. "Uncle Ethan says we get to go Christmas tree hunting. You can come, too."

"Christmas tree hunting, huh? Sounds fun," Julian said.

Ethan ruffled the top of Andrew's head and passed him a wool cap. "Your sister will tan both our hides if you lose another hat." To Rachel, Ethan said, "Andrew and Jacob saw you from the wagon on the ride in. Every year we help find a Christmas tree for the center of town. Brenna talked Brody and Katharine away from the clinic long enough to help."

"You get to come, too, and you, Mr. Frank." Andrew clasped Rachel's hand, and the smile she wore was of genuine affection for the boy, making Julian wonder just how much time she spent at the ranch for them to have become such close friends.

Rachel's eyes met Julian's, and he allowed himself a few seconds before answering her unasked question. "I don't imagine you did too much Christmas tree hunting in San Francisco." Julian couldn't lay claim to ever selecting a holiday tree, either. His holiday history didn't resemble those in the tales written by the likes of Dickens, Moore, and Irving.

"No, someone always delivered the tree." She tilted her head slightly toward the meadow. "You had something more to show me, I think."

"It'll keep." Julian bent forward enough to look Andrew in the eye. "Looks like you have two more tree hunters if you'll have us."

In answer, Andrew pulled on Rachel's hand and began reciting everything he knew about the best trees. Not to be left out, little Jacob wiggled in his father's arm until Ethan set him down so he could reach for Rachel's other hand and walk alongside them.

Rachel soon sat on a bench padded with blankets, inside what looked more like a wagon attached to runners than the sleek sleighs and cutters she'd seen in catalogs and advertisements.

Someone built two benches close to the front, with a third bench built higher for the driver. Katharine and Brody shared one bench, while young Jacob kept trying to stand up between Rachel and Julian. With a laugh, Julian kept two steady hands on Jacob to keep him from wobbling while the young boy clapped as the horses carried them through the snow. Andrew held the reins, under Ethan's close guidance, and led the sleigh toward a thick stand of trees near the road.

With the sleigh stopped adjacent to the tree line, everyone disembarked. While Brody helped his wife out, Julian lifted Jacob to the ground. Once the little boy hurried to his father and cousin, Julian turned back to the sleigh. "May I?"

Rachel saw no other way down and nodded. Julian's hands circled her waist and she placed hers on his shoulders for support. In seconds, her feet were on solid ground and she smiled. "That wasn't so hard." Realizing she spoke the words aloud, Rachel added, "I did not mean to say . . . what I meant . . ."

"I know what you meant." Julian brushed a snowflake from her nose before it could melt. "And no, it wasn't so hard." He smiled and waited for her to walk ahead of him. Katharine invited Rachel to join her, while Brody and Julian examined a few nearby pines and Ethan explained to Jacob why they couldn't cut down the biggest tree in the woods.

Katharine waited until they were far enough from the others before softly asking, "I realize when people say they do not want to pry that they really do, so please tell me if I am crossing a line in our friendship."

Rachel's laugh was as soft as Katharine's whispered words. "It will be easier if you simply ask what you want to know."

"Is all well between you and Julian? Only, I heard what you said when he lifted you from the sleigh."

"I thought the words were only in my mind, and then he heard . . . well, it does not matter." Rachel gave a gentle tug to a branch within easy reach and watched it spring back. "All is well between me and

Julian. He asked permission before touching me. Everyone did for a long time, women included, even for a simple handshake, until you all gradually stopped. Did I behave differently? I do not know, but he—" Rachel looked at Julian, "still asks."

"Have you spoken to him about it?"

Rachel shook her head. "I never imagined I would welcome another man's touch after what happened with Slade Ryker, or that a man might . . ." She faced her friend. "Slade is dead now. That is what Julian wanted to tell me. And now look at you, ready to cry."

Katharine looped an arm through Rachel's. "As horrific as my reasoning may be, I am sad and happy all at once, and my brain and heart cannot agree on how to manifest both emotions. But if you wish it, then I will stop at once."

Rachel's next laugh drew the others' attention, though only Julian's gaze lingered on her.

Brody called out, "We all have different opinions on the best tree. We need you fine ladies to settle things so we can get out of the snow before we all freeze."

"Shall we help them?" Katharine asked.

"I think we shall." It was Rachel who took the first step toward the others, though her eyes never turned away from Julian's. "Now, what are the choices?"

Andrew pointed to his tree first, a pine so massive and a crown so high up it appeared to reach the clouds. Jacob's enthusiastic clapping from Ethan's arms indicated his approval of Andrew's choice. "Yes, well, that is quite a tree. It is a shame, though, that we wouldn't be able to put a star on top."

Andrew peered up as high as the surrounding trees allowed. "We have to have a star on top."

"I cannot imagine a ladder high enough to reach the top, or anywhere close to it." Rachel brushed her hand along the branches at the base. "But the town can decorate near the bottom and still make it quite festive, I'm sure."

Jacob seemed to sense his cousin's hesitation now. When Andrew did not comment for several seconds, Jacob pointed and said, "Our tree!"

"Maybe the tree Doc Brody picked instead," Andrew finally said.

Everyone gave Brody's choice for the town's tree a fair appraisal before nodding. Katharine traded Rachel's arm for her husband's. "A fine choice."

Andrew walked over to give Brody's tree a better examination. He then pointed to another tree a few feet away, tucked against a massive trunk. It stood tall, perhaps seven feet, with a bent and twisted trunk and branches too weak to hold more than a few ribbons. "That's the one Julian picked."

"It looks in need of a second chance." Julian shrugged and lifted one of two axes from the back of the wagon and handed one to Brody. "Doc, your choice it is. You do the honors."

Brody winked at his wife, checked to make sure everyone was far out of range from his swing and brought arm and axe around to make the first cut. He and Julian made quick work of cutting through the trunk and loading it into the wagon. The top half hung out the back, and Rachel imagined their group of tree hunters made for a merry picture as the sleigh carried them back toward town.

She leaned forward to ask Ethan, "How did you get the task of helping to select the tree this year?"

Ethan smiled. "You mean because there are so many of us Gallaghers now?"

Rachel blushed a little and nodded.

"They'll all come to town for the decorating, and this year, the party at the inn on Christmas Eve. Victoria has been fussy and Brenna didn't want to leave her today, Isabelle and Gabriel are spending some extra time with their baby daughter, and Ramsey and Eliza are treating a horse with a sprained leg. Besides, it's Jacob's first Christmas tree hunt."

Ethan's loving look at his son, who sat next to Julian, warmed every corner of her heart. She understood exactly why Ethan Gallagher, head of the family, and a man plenty to keep him busy from dawn to dusk, walked away from it all to watch the joy on his son's face.

Rachel sat back and shared a soft smile with Julian, who held onto Jacob while the little boy slept.

With fresh air in her lungs and a new memory to keep her thoughts occupied the remainder of the afternoon, Rachel said goodbye to her friends and returned to the inn. After kicking snow off her boots and removing the rest of her outer clothing once inside the kitchen, she mentally ticked off what she still had to accomplish.

Katharine suggested Rachel enjoy the

rest of the day on her own time, and she considered it, but with so much left to do, Rachel preferred to get a few more things done today. Besides, she worked through problems better when she kept busy. Tomorrow, when the town came together to decorate the tree, would be soon enough for her to be surrounded by people. For now, she enjoyed the quiet.

"Miss Watson?"

Rachel almost jumped from where she stood at the sound of Hugh Peterson's voice. It took her brain a moment to recognize it as his. She composed herself before facing the craftsman.

"I'm real sorry, Miss Watson." He hurried into the kitchen and moved one of his custom chairs next to her. "You go on and have a seat there if you feel a spell coming on."

A spell? Rachel must have looked worse than she felt if Hugh thought she was going to faint. She braced an arm on the table's edge to prove she could still stand. "It is quite all right. I was woolgathering and did not hear anyone else about."

Hugh nodded in understanding. Of course, he and everyone else who was around last year when she showed up in Briarwood knew at least part of her story.

"I reckon we all daydream now and again. Would you like some water?"

Uncertain if he'd leave her alone until she assured him she was fine, Rachel nodded. "Thank you, that would be kind." Rachel drank a third of the water from one of the new glasses Katharine had ordered. "Just what I needed after all the fresh air today."

"Well, it's a fine day for it now that the sun's out. We'll get more snow tonight, though."

Rachel released her grip on the water glass as her body relaxed. "Were you looking for me earlier or Katharine?"

"Yes, ma'am. That is, either of you, ma'am. We put the last bed together upstairs. The builders said they could finish up around it. They're all done in the dining room, so we delivered the sideboard. The boys and I will be back next week, after the builders are done, to make sure all the furniture is right where you want it, and to deliver the rest of the tables and chairs."

Rachel mustered enough strength to follow Hugh into the dining room. The long, mahogany piece with rosewood inlay was two individual sideboards set together, per Katharine's request. It filled a good portion of the south wall. Though simple in design, the craftsmanship rivaled the one from the mansion where Rachel had worked in the city. The wood gleamed, and they had carved each drawer handle into pine branches, with detail so fine she touched one to ensure herself they weren't real. "You have a gift, Mr. Petersen. A beautiful gift. Katharine will be pleased."

"Thank you, kindly, Miss Watson." Hugh pulled a wool cap from his back pocket. "I'd best get back to the farm. I gave all my workers tomorrow off on account of the tree decorating."

"You have worked wonders, and Katharine wouldn't expect any of you to miss tomorrow's enjoyments." Rachel breathed deeply and held out her hand. Surprised, Hugh accepted and shook. "Thank you for all of your hard work."

"Thank you, ma'am."

With a wide smile, Hugh left out the back door. Rachel took her time and ran her fingertips over the top of the smooth wood. When she returned to the kitchen, she picked up the glass to wash it at the sink, but her legs carried her no farther than the table. Rachel lowered herself onto the high-backed wooden chair and stared at nothing.

"Rachel?"

She looked up, though did not immediately acknowledge Julian's presence in the doorway. He quickly closed the kitchen door against rising winds. When had it started to snow again? "I only took a moment to rest." Rachel stood and walked to the stove, checked the fire inside to make sure there was still enough heat, and filled the kettle with fresh water. "Would you like tea?"

"Better not. With the weather brewing, I came over to walk you back to the general store." Julian brushed a little snow off his arms and remained by the door. "I figured you'd be about done now. Katharine was worried."

"Quite well, thank you. Of course, I'm not done. I've only been here a short while, since we came back from our excursion. I'll be a few hours . . . what do you mean you thought I'd be done?"

Julian shrugged out of his coat and hung it next to his hat before taking a few steps inside the kitchen. "We returned two hours ago, Rachel." He took the kettle off the heat. "What happened?"

"I'm not sure. Two hours?"

"That's right. We got the tree up in the center of town and then the sun moved behind dark clouds, so Ethan took Andrew and Jacob back to the ranch. Wind picked up about fifteen minutes ago, and the snow a few minutes later." Julian cupped her chin and turned her face toward him. "Whatever it is, I hope you'll let me help you."

"I remember nothing after Hugh Petersen left. I sat down to think and . . . then we're here."

Julian dropped his hand to his lap. "They must have been some powerful thoughts."

"It frightened me when Hugh came into the kitchen. With all the quiet, I did not hear him until he spoke. It has been almost two months since the last time, and I assumed it was over now." Rachel heard her rambling words and hoped she made some sense.

"What happened last time?"

"Late one night at the store, I went downstairs to make sure we locked everything up. Loren forgets sometimes. It must have been after nine o'clock, so only shadows and moonlight greeted me. I like it, though, all the quiet at night. Loren was in his back office, and I didn't hear him come through." Rachel shook away what she considered nonsense musings. "You ought to think me feebleminded about now."

"That is the last thing I think of you."

"You always make noise." Rachel stared at him. "Always. In the church, you made certain the sound of your boots alerted me before you ever spoke. You ask before touching me."

Julian cradled her hand in his.

"Most of the time."

He smiled at that. "It should always be your choice."

"I do not mind, you know, when you touch me. I am not so fragile as you might imagine."

"Never crossed my mind that you're feebleminded or fragile." He stood, and she followed. "We need to head out before we can't see a foot in front of us."

Rachel bundled into her outer clothing again. "What about the stove?"

"What's left of the fire will die down on its own." Julian slipped into his coat and hat.

Rachel took a key off a small hook on the wall. "Will we still decorate the tree tomorrow, do you think?"

"Not unless a miracle blows this weather away during the night." He took the key from her and opened the door. They huddled outside, keeping their backs to the wind while Julian locked up and returned the key to Rachel. "Stay close."

Rachel nodded and braced herself. She welcomed Julian's arm around her, and the protection of his taller body as they forged a path the short distance to the general store. The bell jingled when they entered and clanged upon closing.

"Good heavens, dear." Joanna hurried to Rachel's side, her gait surprisingly strong. "I fretted until Brody came by and assured us that Mr. Frank had you well in hand. We have some of Tilly's stew warming on the stove. Plenty for you both."

"Thank you, but I should head out, and shouldn't you still be in bed?"

"I've rested plenty. Will we see you at the tree decorating?" Joanna peered out a window. "Well, in a few days perhaps."

"I'll be there."

Joanna patted him on the arm and said her goodbyes. "Rachel, dear, the stew is in the kitchen. Loren is working on one of his carvings and will enjoy your company."

When Joanna left them alone, Rachel asked Julian, "You'll still be here in a few days?"

He pointed over his shoulder. "Not exactly traveling weather."

"Of course." How foolish for her to imagine he might *want* to stay in Briarwood. "Before Andrew recruited us to hunt for trees, you had something else to tell me."

"I did. I do. Gabriel approached me the other night at Tilly's and mentioned there'd be a sheriff vacancy opening soon."

Rachel nodded. "I heard Tom Carver plans to leave after Christmas. There isn't an official town council or mayor, so it generally falls on the Gallagher family to see to such matters." She explained, "What I do not hear from helping at the store, I learn from Joanna or Loren. It is amazing what people will talk about while they wait for their purchases to be boxed." Rachel chided herself for rambling and willed herself to be quiet.

Julian interrupted her silent admonishment. "Ramsey explained how the town operates when he first asked for my help."

"You mean when he asked you to help find Mary."

"Yes."

"Ramsey," Rachel began, "knew what he was doing. Are you considering the job?"

"I have a job. One I'm good at."

"Yes, you are." In the most private recesses of Rachel's heart, she longed for Julian to stay, though she lacked the courage to tell him. She despised her weakness, her fear, and all the unknowns that came with risking one's heart. "To give up the excitement and adventure you are used to, well, it is a lot for Gabriel—for anyone—to ask."

Wind rattled windows and howled with each gust of blinding snow. "Those were two good reasons why I joined up with the Pinkertons, but not the only ones." He leaned against a wall and stared at the growing blizzard through a window. "One of the boys in the home where I grew up got himself into trouble. Barely fourteen and accused of helping to rob a bank two towns over. No one believed the orphan when the bank teller swore the boy was one of the thieves that rode off with the money."

Rachel puzzled over what Julian was not saying, but she held her questions and let him continue. He watched the snow as if in a daze.

"Boone was his name, though not the one his mother gave him." Julian smiled at the memory. "He said it suited him better than Jedidiah. I believed him. My word didn't carry any clout, being from the same home, and they carted Boone off to the nearest house of refuge. I had the misfortune once of visiting the New York House of Refuge. Overcrowded halls and overworked juveniles. Six months later, after Boone was taken away, the leader of the robbers died and a witness finally came forward. She'd been too afraid of retaliation before. She saw every man who rode away that day, and Boone wasn't among them. He'd simply been nearby when the ruckus happened."

Julian finally looked her way. "Boone died a few weeks later after the witness testified. He's the reason I became a Pinkerton. I didn't trust the so-called system of justice, and thought, maybe, I could do some good for innocent people like Boone." He returned to her side and cupped one side of her face. "People like you and your sister." Julian dropped his hand, brushing over her arm before it landed at his side. "Never think, though, that duty is the only reason why I went after Slade Ryker."

Without another word, Julian opened the door and left the store. Rachel suppressed the urge to follow him into the darkness swirling with snow and air so cold she wondered how anything survived a Montana winter. She thought of the warm stew waiting to be eaten and remembered she had neglected food since breakfast.

An eerie shatter of glass and wood shook the building and halted her steps. "That is not a good sound."

Enough snow fell during the storm to ensure locals throughout the valley would have to dig themselves out for many more days to come. Three days later, when the clouds finally cleared away to reveal pristine blue skies, half the townspeople carried burdens of the labor to the center of the main thoroughfare. Small piles of debris from fallen branches and roof shingles to sections of tree trunks and broken timber and glass filled carts and wagons. While most of the town made it through the storm unscathed, the blizzard left parts of it battered. Two horse-drawn snowplows cleared the road enough for wagons to pass through town and allowed people to move about.

The inn was one of the lucky structures to survive without a blemish, as did Doc Brody's clinic and Tilly's Café. A final tally revealed five homes in town suffered some destruction, though nothing catastrophic. Those who needed roof repairs or window replacements found temporary shelter in the almost-finished rooms of Briarwood's new inn or the rooms above the clinic.

Doc Brody, Ramsey, Hugh Petersen, and half a dozen other men left when the sun came up to see how families, farms, and small homesteads beyond the town fared.

Presently, Katharine's builder, Emmett, who Julian met on his last stop through Briarwood, spoke with Gabriel and Otis about two of the other buildings in need of as much repair as the general store.

Julian stepped off the top rung of the livery's tallest ladder onto the general store's second-level balcony. Sunlight beat down as warm breath met frigid air to create tiny puffs of fleeting mist. Ethan climbed up next and surveyed the damage.

"Well, the tree didn't destroy the support beams, but with all the snow that found a way inside, the floor will have to be replaced." The balcony beneath the two grown men shifted a few inches. "Loren and Joanna aren't going to like it, but they'll have to stay at the inn for another week until the structure is safe. At least the main store was spared."

"How about Hawk's Peak?" Julian recalled a dozen or more men and women called the ranch home, not to mention the children. "Can the ranch do without you,

Gabriel, and Ramsey at the same time?"

Ethan nodded. "We made it through intact, as did all the buildings and almost all the livestock. We lost three head of cattle who wandered from the herd. It could have been a lot worse for everyone. Besides, these people are like family, too."

Julian saw Rachel stepping onto the front porch of the inn to help Tilly pass out mugs of coffee, cocoa, and cider to workers. Some ventured into the café when they'd been outside for too long, but not much time would pass before they got back to work.

She forgot her hat again, he mused. The golden locks were braided and twisted together at the nape, with a few loose strands framing her face. Rachel remembered her scarf, and out of habit, Julian looked down at the boots peeking out from beneath her long skirts when she moved. He ought to get her a pair of the fur-lined moccasins favored by many people of the tribal nations and every mountain man he'd ever met, and then wondered if any cobbler would make such a thing for a woman.

"Julian?"

He tore his gaze from Rachel and addressed Ethan. "What did you ask?"

Ethan looked to where Julian's attention had been. "Have you given any thought to staying? The sheriff's job is a legitimate offer." He called out a warning to clear the area before dropping a large branch to the ground below. "The worst of things died away with Nathan Hunter. We don't see as much crime in Briarwood these days, but we can't control who comes and goes."

Julian suspected they were both thinking about Slade Ryker and others like him. Ramsey had given him a general idea of what the Gallagher family, and the people of Briarwood, had suffered through when Nathan Hunter was alive. Julian had heard plenty more about Hunter and the men who once worked for him, taking money in exchange for tormenting innocent people.

Men like Hunter and Ryker served the world better where they now lay—dead and buried.

Ethan continued, drawing Julian from his mental wanderings. "With the spur line, we've already seen more people travel through this valley."

Julian pulled a branch from the broken window in what used to be Rachel's bedroom and tossed it below. "I have given many hours of thought to the offer."

"You'd make more staying with the Pinkertons—"

"It's not the money."

"For most men, it would be."

Most men had families to support, Julian thought, or if single, spent hard-earned coin on gambling and carousing. Julian lived simply, which meant he survived on a fraction of his current salary and saved the rest. He sometimes pictured a home and family, but the wife and children of his imaginings had no faces, until now. "It's not the money." He dropped two more branches to the ground and watched Rachel walk back into the inn.

"Any unfinished business with the Pinkertons or anywhere else?"

"Not anymore."

Ethan pushed against the remainder of the aspen that lay half inside Rachel's bedroom. "A saw should cut through the rest of this quickly enough." He stood up and once more followed Julian's line of sight. "I've had the honor to give a few friends advice, hoping they avoid my mistakes when it came to courting the women who are now their wives." He slapped the side of Julian's arm to gain his attention. "Don't wait to tell her how you feel."

"What mistakes?"

"Suffice to say I had to travel to Scotland to get Brenna back. We were both stubborn, proud, and determined to wait until the other flinched. I almost made the biggest mistake of my life letting her go." Ethan crossed the balcony to the ladder.

"Everyone who has spent more than half an hour with me comes to know that I prefer my ranch to town and my family to the company of anyone else. A person might mistake that to mean I don't keep watch on what goes on everywhere else. Rachel has found a new home in Briarwood, which I suspect you've already figured out."

"Meaning?"

Ethan started down the ladder. "Meaning, you won't have to travel as far as San Francisco. She's only a short walk away."

Julian took Ethan's counsel under advisement during the next five days. With all the cleanup needed around town and at a few of the homesteads on the outskirts, storm damage kept him and every other man busy hauling and hammering. He saw Rachel only from a distance as she kept busy with the unexpected early guests at the inn.

After a decade of traveling by horse,

stage, and train, it felt good to repair and build something tangible. Swinging a hammer or grinding a saw blade through wood used neglected muscles. When Julian stepped up to the kitchen door at The Briarwood Inn, more than a few of those muscles ached for a hot bath. The room above Brody's clinic was a comfortable place to lay his head after a long day, but it wouldn't work permanently.

He considered the rooms above the jail against all the trappings of the new hotel. Part of considering the offer to become Briarwood's new sheriff meant weighing every pro and con. After a week of deliberations, every scenario he conjured ended with the need for one thing— Rachel.

"Six days until Christmas."

"We'll make it!" Katharine set the last

serving platter in one of the two kitchen storage hutches.

"I am sorry you didn't get to keep the interior a surprise until the grand opening. It has been helpful, though, to test our skills." Rachel set out fresh muffins from Tilly's on a plate alongside fresh-brewed tea. "A person should learn early on that they cannot cook."

"Breakfast was not that bad."

Rachel's raised brow suggested otherwise. "I burned everything. Were it not for Joanna taking over the first morning, our guests would have starved. You mentioned a plan, and while the anticipation has been fun, it is time to unveil this mysterious cook."

Katharine's laugh filled the kitchen. "You are about to enjoy one of the cook's delicious muffins."

"Tilly is going to cook for the inn?" Rachel waited for Katharine to sit before joining her and pouring the tea. "What about her café?"

"Not exactly. We came to an arrangement, Tilly and I, not only to ensure she does not lose business. but also so we can provide all the conveniences of on-site meals to our guests. She will prepare most everything at her café, or the start of everything—stews, pies, loaves of bread, and such—and then we will cook or bake it here. She gives us a discount and we give our guests wonderful food. Tilly's niece is a fair cook, so she will run the kitchen here. We realize the arrangement will not work indefinitely, but for the first winter, when business is slow, it should work well."

Rachel bit into an apple and spice muffin and closed her eyes in pleasure. "May I ask you a question? One I have wanted to ask for a while now."

"Of course."

"Why build a hotel here? I understand why you stayed in Briarwood, because of Brody, but why the financial risk of a small hotel in a mountain town that barely warrants a marking on territorial maps?"

Katharine sipped her tea before answering. "You are not the first to ask. Brody was certainly the reason I stayed, and I could have happily lived as a doctor's wife. The inn is because of my mother and father. I remember one winter when bitter, icy winds swept off the ocean, frosting over all it touched. A young family—the parents were your age—and the three children between ages four and ten, were new to the area and unprepared. My parents welcomed these strangers into our home, gave them a warm place to stay, and invited them to dine at our table.

"When the storm passed two days later, the family left with warmer clothes for the children and the husband a better job working for my father. The looks on their faces when they left my parents' home were of wonderment. They had been treated as friends and sent away in better spirits than when they arrived. I never forgot them or my parents' kindness."

Rachel's tea and half a muffin remained

untouched while she listened and considered. "And you wanted to see that look again."

Katharine nodded. "Time and time again. It will not always be so easy, and we are certain to have the occasional guest who tries our patience, but traveling, even for all its enjoyment, is difficult. Most people miss home and family, and if we can help lighten the journey of even one traveler, then it will be well worth it."

The following morning, all of the temporary guests, including Loren and Joanna, left the inn. Rachel did not return with them. She had moved into the comfortable room off the kitchen, and after Julian and Emmett salvaged what they could from her room above the general store, she found the new space suited her, and her new role as manager of The Briarwood Inn.

It was five days until Christmas and just as many days since she had last seen Julian ride out of town toward Hawk's Peak.

Rachel restrained her wandering thoughts and smiled as she fluffed the pillows on her bed and smoothed a few wrinkles from the quilt. No matter what happened from this moment on, she vowed to always find a reason to smile.

"Rachel?"

It was not the familiar voice she had hoped to hear, but she kept the smile in place and walked into the kitchen. Brody stood just inside the door, in the same place Julian opted to stand when he didn't want to track snow inside. The thick rug Rachel placed there kept the wood beneath from soiling and warping.

"This is a pleasant surprise. Just last night Katharine said you delivered two more babies this week and tended a family near the old mine."

"A boy and girl, twins and both healthy." Brody removed his hat and kept close to his side. "Two families are still living near the mine. The men are cousins and brought their families here because of the work. It will be a hard winter if they decide to stay up there any longer."

"Would you like some tea or coffee?" Rachel motioned him farther inside.

"Thank you, but I'll be going back out soon." He peered down at his boots and grinned. "And Katharine would tan me good if I ruined the new floors. I've come on another matter." Brody slipped a letter from his pocket and passed it to Rachel. "That arrived inside of a letter addressed to me and Katharine. It came on the train before the storm hit, and Otis just drove out to the spur station yesterday to pick up the mail and supplies that were left."

Rachel turned it over and immediately recognized the fine script. "This is from Mary."

Brody nodded. "She wrote to thank us and asked me and Katharine to look after you. She also asked me to deliver her letter to you."

"I don't understand. Why include it with yours rather than yours with mine?" Rachel and Mary's aunt was not wealthy, but extra postage would not be the reason for her sister's decision.

"Mary indicated the reason is in her letter."

"Thank you, Brody." Rachel pressed the envelope to her heart. She did not know what to expect from her sister after informing Mary that she planned to remain in Briarwood.

Brody put his hat back on and extended his and Katharine's invitation to dine with them that evening. "Katharine is trying a roast chicken recipe that Elizabeth gave her. Five o'clock?"

Elizabeth, Brenna and Ramsey's grandmother, made sandwiches from roast chicken once when Rachel was visiting Hawk's Peak. "If it is Elizabeth's recipe, then I've no doubt it will taste delicious. I accept the invitation, and thank you both for it."

"You are family and always welcome." Brody tapped the brim of his hat in farewell before letting himself out the door.

Family, Rachel thought, and studied the envelope once more. Given the choice, she would have closed herself away in her new room and given the letter immediate attention. Instead, she found herself busy soon after Brody left.

Hugh Petersen delivered the remaining furniture, as promised. Katharine sent a note around that she would arrive late, with only an explanation that Brody needed unexpected help at the clinic. Once all the furniture was placed, Rachel thanked Hugh and handed him an envelope Katharine left for him.

"I've already been paid, Miss Watson."

Rachel folded his hand over it. "Katharine said it's a Christmas bonus for you and your employees. Your work, Hugh . . ." Rachel looked around to admire the craftsmanship in every piece once more. "Rivals some of the finest I've ever seen. You have earned it."

"It has been an honor and pleasure, Miss

Watson. I'll be sure to give my thanks to Mrs. Brody when I see her next." He held up the envelope. "This'll help the men and their families through the winter."

"Before you leave . . ." Rachel asked him to follow her into the kitchen where she kept pencil and paper to write out lists. "Could you make me something?" She drew a rough sketch and showed him the paper. "I lack the artistic talent to provide more detail."

"Oh, I see it just fine, Miss Watson. How big are you wanting it?"

Rachel created a box in the air with her hands, then widened them a bit. "About this big. It will be a gift, so I prefer no one else know about it."

"For Christmas?" Hugh asked.

"I do not expect it to be done that soon."

"I can if you want it."

Rachel did not wish to take advantage of the man's kindness, though in the end, she nodded. "If it's possible, then yes, I would be grateful."

"Sure thing, Miss Watson."

Hugh left and Tilly and her niece arrived to discuss the menu for the inn's Christmas party and to get better acquainted with the kitchen. Three hours later, after two cups of tea and one of Tilly's sinful flaked-crust pastries filled with berries she had preserved in summer, she said goodbye once more.

A glance at the clock revealed she had little time to get ready for dinner with the Brody's. Her wardrobe comprised only a few dresses warm enough for winter, and while her savings, accumulated from years as a governess, was enough to see her clothed, fed, and housed for at least a long winter, she did not wish to squander the hard-earned money on frivolities. She decided her friends would not mind if she didn't change for supper.

Another knock had Rachel bowing her head in a silent prayer that whoever stood on the other side would make their visit quick. She opened the door, surprised to see Forest Lloyd, son of the telegraph operator and postmaster, holding a large, semi-flat rectangular package. "Come inside, Forest. What is this?"

"Package arrived for Mrs. Brody. The sign on the clinic door says the Doc's with a patient, and no one answered at their house. Pa figured I should bring it here."

"Of course. You can set it on the table, and I will let Mrs. Brody know it is here."

"Thanks, Miss Watson!" The young man set his burden on the long kitchen table and said goodbye.

Rachel examined the package for any sign of its origins. They were not expecting any extra supplies for the inn until after Christmas, and the simple, brown wrapping showed only an origin address from Denver. She debated taking it with her to supper, but if Brody and Katharine were still—

"Rachel?"

She recognized the voice she had waited for but not heard in five days. Rachel opened the door to Julian and stepped back to let him inside. "You're still here."

Julian heard the surprise in her voice. "Where else would I be?" He brushed past that question to comment, "The tree looks great. I'm sorry I missed it."

"The townspeople put on quite a showing. I have seen nothing like it before."

"Rachel?" He tipped her face up with a knuckle beneath her chin. "What's wrong?"

She cleared her throat.

"I thought you had left."

"I'd never leave town without saying goodbye."

Rachel gripped the back of a chair. "Then you are leaving."

"A telegram came from the Pinkertons. They have a new assignment for me."

"When do you leave?"

"That's what I want to talk to you about. Well, one of the things. I stopped at the Brodys before coming to see you, and they mentioned supper. I'll walk you over and then we can talk tomorrow."

Rachel took her coat and scarf down from the hooks. "It is not far for me to walk alone."

"No, it's not." Julian stopped her from wrapping the scarf around her neck a second time. "This is not how I imagined this going, Rachel."

She dropped her hands and peered up at him. "What do you mean?"

"Tomorrow will be better when we're—"

"Please, tell me. What is it you want?"

"To love you." The words slipped off his tongue as though they'd been there for months and had grown tired of waiting.

"You don't mean it."

A scorching knife could not have caused as much pain as the look of disbelief Rachel wore. Words and promises of love were not part of his life, for not once had he uttered them to another person. Julian knew he'd never say them to another woman.

"Trust is hard to come by, and I don't expect—"

"I trust you, Julian. I have always trusted you, but love . . ."

"It's all right." He cupped her face. "It's all right." Julian stepped away from her. "We'd better go before Katharine sends Brody to find out what's keeping us."

"Julian."

He tried to keep his voice light and his smile sincere when he held out his hand. "Tomorrow."

Rachel accepted and together they left the inn.

Julian accepted Katharine's invitation to dine with them, for no other reason than to convince Rachel that he was not upset with her. She darted glances his way throughout the meal, and when dessert was offered, Julian suffered through it. If anyone noticed how little he spoke, they did not comment.

Two and a half hours later, he walked Rachel back to the inn and declined her offer for tea. "I need to see if Orin is still at the telegraph office."

"You're not taking the sheriff's job then?"

"It's not a good idea." Julian backed away.

"Why not?"

"Tomorrow, Rachel."

"Julian, please. Don't leave angry."

He closed his eyes for a second before stepping onto the porch again. "I'm not angry." Julian held her hands and lifted their joined grasp between them. "I will always watch over you, but I can't stay close, be in Briarwood every day, wanting what I want—wanting you. It was unfair of me, what I said earlier tonight." Respect and love for her kept Julian from kissing her upturned mouth. Instead, he released her hands. "I'll stay for Christmas."

He walked into the darkness, never looking back, and kept walking until the outline of the small church came into view. Julian stared at it for several minutes before entering the structure.

The air inside held a touch of frost. Julian sat in a pew near the front, where moonlight shined through a window and illuminated slivers of the interior. It lacked the ethereal effect he remembered when Rachel had sat in the same pew and sunlight filtered over her.

The door opened, and a burst of cold followed Reverend Philips down the aisle. "Thought I saw someone come this way. Mind if I join you?"

Julian sat straighter in the pew. "Not at all." He recalled the reverend lived in one of the houses that made it through the storm unscathed. "We haven't officially met. Julian Frank."

"Oh, I know who you are, Mr. Frank. You're a bit of a hero in these parts."

"I'm no one's hero, and please, it's Julian. What takes you out into the cold night?"

"Never miss a nightly walk." The reverend chuckled. "Well, make one or two nights, when we get weather as bad as the storm that passed through. I like to make sure folks are tucked in at night before I find my own bed."

Amused with the older man, Julian asked, "And the folks who find the saloon friendlier than their homes?"

"Them, too." The reverend's wide smile lit up his entire face and animated warm, brown eyes. "What brought you to the church tonight?"

"It's warmer in here than out there."

Reverend Philips laughed again. "Certainly is. There's more than one direction to walk, yet you came here."

He eyed the reverend, admiring the man's unflinching expression and genuine interest. Reading people well and fast had made Julian a worthy opponent to every person he tracked and helped bring to justice. The instinct told him when someone was guilty or innocent, or if they wanted information of their own. His read on the good reverend was that the man cared more about the person than the answer to a single question. "Faith is a never-ending journey. That's what you tell people, right?"

Reverend Philips nodded. "I recall saying those exact words to Miss Watson recently." He found a more comfortable position and rested an arm over the back of the pew. "Do you not agree?"

"Makes enough sense for me to believe it."

"You're struggling with something."

Julian met the reverend's stare. "Never met a person who wasn't." He leaned forward, resting elbows on knees. The pews were low enough so he could still see over the one in front of him. "A choice."

"Between what?"

"Pain comes with either one, so it's more a matter of choosing between the lesser of two miseries."

Reverend Philips pointed to the window. "You happen to be sitting in one of my favorite spots. No matter the time of day, season, or weather, a sliver of sun or moon finds a way through and touches right where you are."

Julian looked around and saw that other than a single pew, the rest of the church was dark, like the clouds covering the valley outside. He honestly did not know what he was supposed to think or say in response.

"You see, Mr. Frank, it is a reminder that all we ever have to do is look up to know we aren't alone and look within to find the answers we seek."

Up and within. Not exactly the answer I expected. Julian kept the thoughts to himself.

"You said you are no one's hero." Reverend Philips stretched his long legs and stood. "Can't say I agree, and neither does Miss Watson. You did more than save her sister. You saved Rachel."

Julian shook his head. "She saved herself." And no—no one—would ever say differently and get away with it. Not around him. "She saved herself, Reverend."

"She did that and more. Sit there a while and think on it." He patted Julian's shoulder and left the same way he came.

"Rachel saved herself." A curse almost slid off his tongue. "Sorry about that," he said to the church. Julian wanted to stay, put down those roots people talk about, and build a life on more than passing acquaintances. A cold bed under a blanket of stars was worth it when the quest ended with true justice service. Except, he began to imagine life could be more.

His hands carried the stain of blood beneath them, and those deaths remained imprinted on his soul. Not a single choice did he regret, but a woman like Rachel deserved a man untainted.

Julian's gaze lifted again to the window, then back to the pew. He saw Rachel sitting there as if she really sat beside him in a halo of moonlight. Beautiful, kind, and pure. Pure. Understanding came slowly until the force of it tightened his chest and the sensation squeezed his heart.

"This is the most beautiful tree I have ever seen." Rachel set the step ladder aside and stood back with Katharine to admire the results of their labor. "You will have a few surprises for everyone after all." Garlands of pine draped doorways and handrails, each bough selected, gathered, and tied together with their own hands. The new experience was one of many for Rachel this holiday season. A variety of sweet and savory fragrances from the kitchen mingled with the pine and made the whole inn smell like . . . Christmas. Rachel smiled and adjusted a ribbon on the tree. "It is perfect."

Katharine studied the tree this way and that. "Yes, it is. Tilly and her niece have the food well in hand, we decorated every room with as much festive cheer as we can manage, which means there is one thing left to do before the party tonight. Come with me, please."

Bemused, Rachel followed her friend upstairs and down the hall to one of the luxury guest rooms. She waited while Katharine crossed the room and pulled something out from under the bed—the package Forest Lloyd had delivered to the inn. "Why is that up here? I thought Brody took it with him when last he was here."

"Why on earth would he? This is for you."

Rachel walked to Katharine's side. "I do not understand."

"A Christmas gift, Rachel. Tradition demands I wait for this evening or tomorrow, but you will want it before then."

"But I . . . I did not get you anything."

"Your being here is a gift more worthy than anything I can give. For now, allow me the pleasure of watching you open this." Katharine removed the plain brown wrapping to reveal a red box and pushed it across the bed to Rachel. "Go ahead."

Rachel lifted the lid and pulled back the thin muslin fabric. With reverence, she touched the tips of her fingers to the white fabric. "This is too much."

"It most certainly is not." Katharine clapped her hands once. "Please, take it out. I want to see if it as I remember it."

"Remember? When did you—"

Katharine grinned. "When Finn and I were in Denver."

"That was months ago. How could you have known I would still be here?"

"I hoped." Katharine lifted a sleeve and helped Rachel hold it up against her. "It's even lovelier. You will look a vision in it tonight."

"But I can't. I mean, it's . . ." Rachel exhaled a deep breath and smoothed a hand over the bodice. A matching coat in a different shade of white still lay in the box. "This is the most beautiful dress I have ever seen." Appreciating that the gift of giving meant as much to Katharine as the receiving meant to Rachel, she swallowed the lump of pride. "Thank you."

"You are most welcome. Now—"

"Wait." Rachel fingered the locket that once belonged to her mother. She put it in her pocket that morning, not realizing why until now. She withdrew it and showed it to Katharine. "This is the only thing I have left from my life, before." Rachel opened Katharine's hand and placed the locket in her palm.

"You must hold on to it, then."

"Look inside." Katharine flipped open the locket. On one side, a small, dried flower rested. The other side was empty. "I removed the picture and gave it to Mary before she left. The flower, my mother said, is heather and was there when she received it from her mother. It is told that an elderly healer in the Irish mountains gifted the locket with the flower to my grandmother on her wedding day."

Katharine held the gift reverently. "This is precious, Rachel. It is too much."

"No. What I have found here is precious. It once belonged to a healer, and it is fitting that it now be passed on to another. Brody healed my body, but you helped heal my heart. The town and its people, this valley . . . this is my life now. What came before shaped who I am, but I prefer who I am now."

Katharine swiped a tear away and leaned forward to kiss Rachel's cheek. "I will treasure it always." They laughed in joy as Rachel folded the dress back into the box. Studying the locket again, Katharine said, "What about Julian?"

Rachel put the lid back in place and gathered the discarded brown paper.

"Is he part of your life now?"

Rachel thought of the carved box Hugh was making for her—a gift for Julian, a place to store new memories, and prayed she still had a chance to give it to him. "I messed up, Katharine."

"Whatever do you mean?"

"He isn't staying, because of me. I said something I don't think I can take back."

Katharine brought Rachel into a hug. "Somehow I think it is going to take a lot more than a few words to keep Julian Frank away from you."

Light and laughter filled the inn. She worried if those who lived beyond town would make it to the celebration, though she needn't have been concerned. Everyone she'd met in the past year, including many she hadn't, mingled and talked. Gaiety held a firm spot on the menu alongside Tilly's tartlets and pies, meat-filled pastries, and a variety of small cakes.

An hour into the celebration, Rachel

found herself searching each room on the main level once again for Julian. After another half hour and increasing warmth inside, Rachel went to her room to get the new jacket, and sneaked out the back door. The fresh night air cooled her skin and stars twinkled above. So bright was the blanket of sky, she could clearly see the snow-covered mountains bathed by the moon's luminescence.

"You are beautiful."

She took her time to turn her eyes away from the night landscape and rest them on Julian. "You came."

"I gave you my word."

"And you always keep a promise."

Julian nodded and walked to the porch. "Will you walk with me? We won't go far." He held out his hand and waited for her to accept. She did, knowing it was more than a hand he offered. "I meant what I said. You're beautiful."

Rachel smiled, hoping he could see. "The dress—"

"It's pretty, but I said 'you' not the dress."

As promised, he did not lead her far. Faded laughter and conversation reached just beyond the shield of warmth Rachel imagined surrounded them. "Did you truly mean what else you told me?"

He turned her to face him. "I love you, Rachel. Don't ask me to tell you when it happened because I don't know. It's as though what I feel has always been there. When I said I can't stay here, wanting you, and not being with you, I spoke from fear and selfishness. My life has been hard, and some things I've done are unworthy of you. I accepted the job as sheriff."

"Quiet." Rachel shook her head a few times and pressed a palm against his chest. "It is I who felt unworthy."

"You're not—"

Rachel touched a finger to his lips, silencing him. "I accepted that before, up here." She tapped the side of her head. "But I had to accept it here." She touched the place over her heart. "My sister wrote me a letter, and I only read it yesterday. Among other things, she wanted me to tell you again how grateful she is that you came into our lives when you did. She asked me to thank Ramsey for having the intelligence to ask for your help, Brody and Katharine for nursing her back to health, and the Gallaghers and everyone else who befriended her while she was here.

"She knew I wanted to stay, and somehow, Mary knew you would be here still, with me. Mary is wise beyond her years, and wiser than I ever gave her credit. She put the letter in with one she wrote to Brody and Katharine, though her reason for doing so was not immediately apparent."

"What did she write?" Julian asked in a whisper.

"Her exact words were, 'Those with open hearts accept help when given, give help with grace, and remember that no one is ever alone so long as they keep a friend close."'"

"Why did she want Brody or Katharine to deliver it?"

"A reminder, I think, that I need to let others be there for me, which I have learned to do, though it is not always easy. Before . . . Montana, I did not have friends beyond my sister and aunt."

"Someday, I'd like to get to know your sister better and meet your aunt."

Rachel closed the inches between them. "They'll love you."

"Will you let me love you, Rachel? I'll wait, for as long as you need."

"I don't want to wait." She did not possess enough courage to rise and kiss him as she wanted. "I want every Christmas, for the rest of our lives, to be this precious. I'm ready to love you back."

Julian released a shuddering breath and removed his gloves. He held her face, cupped in his palms, skin to skin, and lowered his lips to hers. The kiss lasted seconds, yet held a lifetime of promises.

"Rachel? Julian?"

He kissed her again, this time lingering. Smiles touched them both at the sound of their names called out again. They turned and waved back to Katharine, who called out, "The caroling is about to begin!"

Julian brushed a blond curl away from her cheek and flipped a loose end of her scarf over her shoulder. "I should warn you now, I do not sing."

Rachel kissed his cheek, then his lips, realizing she could never touch him enough, love him enough to satisfy her. "Everyone sings."

"No, they don't."

"Then I will sing, and you can hold my hand."

"With great pleasure, Rachel Watson." They walked side by side back to the inn, to family, and to a new life.

Thank you for reading
Christmas in Briarwood

Did you know there are seven more stand-alone Montana Gallagher novels? Visit mkmcclintock.com for more on the Gallagher family, Hawk's Peak, and Briarwood.

Hungry for more historical adventure, romance, and mystery? Explore MK's other exciting and heartwarming books at her website.

Hear from MK

Want to keep up with MK's new releases? Sign up at
www.mkmcclintock.com/subscribe

ABOUT THE AUTHOR

Award-winning author **MK McClintock** writes historical romantic fiction about chivalrous men and strong women who appreciate chivalry. Her stories of adventure, romance, and mystery sweep across the American West to the Victorian British Isles, with places and times between and beyond. With her heart deeply rooted in the past, she enjoys a quiet life in the northern Rocky Mountains.

Visit MK at **www.mkmcclintock.com**, where you can view all the books, read the blog, explore reader extras, and sign up to receive new release updates.

Made in the USA
Middletown, DE
12 April 2022